● Pl<

THIS WALKER BOOK BELONGS TO:

_____

_____

_____

*For Rita, who first told me about Sam
and for Steve, who takes me sailing
P. R.*

First published as *Sam who was swallowed by a shark*,
1994 by Walker Books Ltd, 87 Vauxhall Walk, London SE11 5HJ

This edition published 2005

2 4 6 8 10 9 7 5 3 1

Text © 1994 Phyllis Root
Illustrations © 1994 Axel Scheffler

The right of Phyllis Root and Axel Scheffler to be identified
as author and illustrator respectively of this work
has been asserted by them in accordance with the
Copyright, Designs and Patents Act 1988

This book has been typeset in Veronan

Printed in China

British Library Cataloguing in Publication Data is available

ISBN 1-84428-557-X

www.walkerbooks.co.uk

SAM
who went to sea

PHYLLIS ROOT

illustrated by AXEL SCHEFFLER

WALKER BOOKS
AND SUBSIDIARIES

LONDON • BOSTON • SYDNEY • AUCKLAND

Sam was a river rat who dreamed of the sea.

At night he heard the
wind in the cottonwoods
and thought of waves
breaking on a faraway shore.

By day he hummed sea shanties as he
tended his garden or mended a fence.

"Better get hammering," old Mr Barleybean said as he passed by one morning. "Fence looks a little rickety."

Sam smiled and nodded and whacked at a nail or two. But soon he was listening again to the river whispering his name.

"Mind those dandelions,"
Mrs Seednibbler warned.
"They're running wild."
Sam tugged at a handful
of weeds, then turned again to stare away
down the river, imagining the sea where
all rivers end.

Not long after, Sam saw an ad in the *Riverside Gazette*.

BUILD YOUR OWN BOAT

GUARANTEED
SEAWORTHY

Your Boat Will Float or Your Money Back

Sam scrimped and pinched and saved and sent away for the plans. At last a package came.

Early next morning, Sam was hammering away in his yard. His neighbours gathered to watch and whisper.

"Funny looking shed," said Mr Barleybean.

"It's not a shed," Sam mumbled through a mouthful of wooden pegs. "It's an ocean-going sailing boat."

"Sam," said Mrs Seednibbler, "this is a little river, a rowing-boat-and-canoe river."

Sam spat the pegs out into his paw. "All rivers lead to the sea," he said. "I have only to follow this one to its end to find my heart's desire."

"Why do you want to go to sea?" demanded old Mr Barleybean.

"It's in my blood," Sam said. "My great-great-great-great-great-great-great grandmother sailed on the *Mayflower*."

"Spring fever, more likely," Mrs Seednibbler muttered. "It will pass."

As the days went by, Sam's boat took shape.

He trimmed the keel,   fitted the ribs,

pegged on the planks,   and laid the deck.

One afternoon, old Mr Barleybean stopped at Sam's gate. "Must be better things to do with your time," he told Sam. "Wash your windows. Trim your hedge. Nail your house down so it won't blow away."

"I want to hear the wind filling my sails," Sam said, pounding in another peg.

Mrs Seednibbler paused on her way to the shop. "A rat was never meant to go to sea," she said. "Rats should have their paws planted firmly on the ground."

"I want to feel the waves rolling under my paws," Sam told her, as he caulked the seams between the planks.

Spring became summer and still Sam worked.

By autumn he was stitching canvas for sails.

His neighbours started to worry in earnest.

"Don't do it, Sam," said old Mr Barleybean. "You'll be attacked by wild seaweed."

"You'll be swallowed by a shark," said Mrs Seednibbler.

"The sea is calling me," Sam said. "It sings to me in my dreams."

Winter came. Sam could be seen through the falling snow, sanding the mast of his boat, his whiskers covered with sawdust and snowflakes.

By spring the boat was ready. Sam named
it *The Rat's Paw* and loaded it with supplies.

His neighbours came to see him off.

Mrs Seednibbler gave him a muffler she had knitted.

Old Mr Barleybean gave him spare nails. "The mast looks a little wobbly," he said.

Sam thanked them all and hugged them goodbye.

"That's the last we'll see of Sam," they told each other, although in their hearts they hoped it wasn't true.

Sam sailed on down the river and into the sea of his heart's desire. The waves sang under him. Storms battered him. The wind pounded his boat. Whales spouted, dolphins leaped and the salt spray matted his fur. At night he munched salt-biscuits and cheese and watched the moon tilt in his sails.

Days ran into weeks and weeks became
months and Sam did not return. Weeds
hid the windows of his house. His chimney
leaned. His neighbours gave up watching
the river for the sight of his mast flying
its bright, brave flag.

"Poor Sam," said old Mr Barleybean. "Tangled up in wild seaweed."

"Poor Sam," said Mrs Seednibbler. "Swallowed by a shark."

One day a passing seagull dropped a note near Sam's house. "Dear friends," Sam's neighbours read. "Please do not worry. I am happy.

Love, Sam."

Far away, out over the water, Sam smiled.
He turned _The Rat's Paw_ seaward and sailed
on and on over the wild green waves.

WALKER BOOKS is the world's leading
independent publisher of children's books.
Working with the best authors and illustrators
we create books for all ages, from babies
to teenagers – books your child will
grow up with and always remember. So…

FOR THE BEST CHILDREN'S BOOKS,
LOOK FOR THE BEAR